Nathaniel Hawthorne, Gabriel Harrison

A Centennial Dramatic Offering

Nathaniel Hawthorne, Gabriel Harrison

A Centennial Dramatic Offering

ISBN/EAN: 9783337343750

Printed in Europe, USA, Canada, Australia, Japan

Cover: Foto ©Andreas Hilbeck / pixelio.de

More available books at **www.hansebooks.com**

A CENTENNIAL DRAMATIC OFFERING.

A ROMANTIC DRAMA,

IN FOUR ACTS, ENTITLED,

THE SCARLET LETTER.

DRAMATIZED FROM NATHANIEL HAWTHORNE'S
MASTERLY ROMANCE.

By GABRIEL HARRISON,

Author of "Life and Writings of John Howard Payne," "The Tragedy
of 'Melanthea'," "The Stratford Bust of Shakespeare," etc.

BROOKLYN, N. Y. :
PRINTED BY HARRY M. GARD[NER]
Corner Court and Joralemon Streets.

ONLY ONE HUNDRED
COPIES PRINTED.

CHARACTERS.

MR. BELLINGHAM, Governor of Boston, Mass.

REV. MASTER ARTHUR DIMMESDALE.

REV. MR. WILSON.

ROGER CHILLINGWORTH.

MASTER TOWNSMAN.

CITIZEN RAWSON.

CAPT. GOODWILL.

WOMEN.

HESTER PRYNNE.

PEARL, Hester's child, seven years old.

MISTRESS HIBBINS, Governor Bellingham's Sister,—A Witch.

MISTRESS GOSSIP.

MISTRESS SMALL.

MARY MERCY, and her little child.

WITCHES AND INDIANS.

SWAMP-FOX—Indian.

SPEAR-HEAD—Indian, belonging to the band of witches.

BLIGHTED-TRUNK—a very old Indian woman, witch.

WEEPING-WILLOW—a young, white girl.

FLEET-WING—Indian.

NIGHT-BIRD—an Indian boy about twelve years old.

Soldiers, Citizens, Sailors, &c., &c.

SCENE, BOSTON, MASS.

Time, 1650. Costumes of the time of King James.

The Scarlet Letter. A. D., 1642.

Hester Prynne, with the letter "A" upon her bosom, and her babe in her arms. is conducted by the Town Beadle from the old Boston Prison to the Penance Scaffold.

Drawn by J. N. Hyde.

SCARLET LETTER.

ACT I.

SCENE FIRST. (In two.)

Exterior of a Prison, painted on flat. The building represents an old-fashioned wooden structure with wooden steps, leading up to an oaken door, with iron cross-bars across the centre. Black backing used. On each side of the door are small windows with iron bars. On the right of the door, painted on the scene, is a rose-bush, in full bloom, running up the face of the house. On each side of the house is a rough stone-wall eight feet high, with sharp iron pickets running along its top. Trees are seen beyond as if standing in the prison yard. The scene is strong in character. A crowd of men, women, squaws and children are discovered standing and sitting around in groups. Mistress Small, Gossip, Mary Mercy, Master Townsman, Rawson and others, standing in centre of stage.

Gossip. Good wives, I'll tell ye a piece of my mind. It would be greatly for the public behoof, if we women, being of mature minds and age, and church-members in good standing, should have the handling of such malefactresses as this Hester Prynne. What think ye, gossips? If the hussy stood up for judgment before us five, that are now here in a knot together, would she come off with such a sentence as the worshipful magistrates have awarded? marry, I trow not!

Small. People say that the Reverend Master Dimmesdale, her godly pastor, takes it very grievously to heart that such a scandal should have come upon his congregation.

Gossip. The magistrates are God-fearing gentlemen, but merciful overmuch,—that is a truth. At the very least, they should have put the brand of a hot iron on Hester

Prynne's forehead. Madam Hester would have winced at that, I warrant me. But she,—the naughty baggage,—little will she care what they put upon the bodice of her gown!—why, look you, she may cover it with a broach, or such like heathenish adornment, and so walk the streets as brave as ever!

Small. Who knows, she may come, stalking out of the prison, with a bunch of flowers covering her brand of shame, so that none of us can see the shape of the letter.

Gossip. A bunch of flowers! The sharpest thorn-apple that ever grew, were too soft and beautiful for the hussy's bosom!

Mercy. O! peace, gentlewomen, let her cover the mark as she will, the pang of it will always be in her heart, and that's enough.

Gossip. I say this woman has brought shame upon us all, and ought to die. Is there not law for it? Truly there is, both in the scripture and the statute-book. Then let the magistrates, who have made these laws of no effect, thank themselves if their own wives and daughters go astray!

Mercy. Good friends, does it follow because one goes unpunished here, that God doth not forgive sin. Better that we should forgive and help Hester out of her troubles. Indeed, Mistress Gossip, you are too hard, and I sorrow for poor Hester.

Gossip. You do! Shame upon you then. Look to the child you hold by the hand; take care her future becomes not like Hester's.

Townsman. Mercy me, good wife, is there no virtue in woman save what springs from a wholesome fear of the gallows?

Mercy. One would think so, master Townsman, the way Mistress Gossip talks.—(The prison-door is heard to unlock, and the chain to fall.) But hush! the lock is turning in the prison-door, and we will soon see Hester Prynne herself, and may-hap some people's hearts will soften a little.

Gossip. Not mine, I warrant you! She should be punished,—but stay! See! The door is open—

The prison-door opens. The Beadle comes down the steps. Hester is seen standing inside of the doorway with her babe in her arms. A ray of light falls across her head and shoulders, which are artistically relieved against the back-ground. A murmur is heard to pass through the crowd, and all push forward to see Hester.

The Beadle with his staff parts the crowd so as to make a centre-opening, that all may see Hester.

Beadle. Room there! make room, and behold Hester Prynne! Room, I say! and behold the Scarlet Letter!

PICTURE. Hester stands for a moment or two inside of the doorway, then steps out upon the upper step. The crowd all stare at her, and whisper to each other.

Mistress Gossip, (*R. C.*) She has good skill in her needle, that's certain, but did any before this brazen hussy, contrive such a way of showing it! Why, gossips, what is it but to laugh in the faces of our own godly magistrates, and make a pride out of what the worthy gentlemen meant for a punishment!

Small. It were well if we stripped Madame Hester's rich gown off of her dainty shoulders; and as for the red letter, which she hath stitched so curiously, I'll bestow a rag of mine own rheumatic flannel to make a fitter one!

Mercy. O! peace! neighbors, peace! do not let her hear you: there is not a stitch in that embroidered letter but what has gone to her very soul.

Beadle, (making gesture with his staff.) Make way, good people! In the King's name, make way! Open a passage, and, I promise ye, Mistress Prynne shall be set where man, woman, and child shall have a fair sight of her brave apparel. A blessing on the righteous colony of the Massachusetts, where iniquity is dragged out into the sunshine! Come along, Madame Hester, and show your scarlet letter in the market-place!

(The people shout "The market-place! The market-place!") The Beadle leads the Procession. Two Soldiers form in front of Hester and two to the rear of her. The people follow.

Beadle. Move on! to the market-place! the market-place! [Excitement. Exeunt crowd, L. H. 1st E.]

Townsman. I feel more sorrow for this woman thus held up to shame before the low rabble, and their vile taunts and sneers, than I could, were she being conducted to death.

Rawson. O far better death, were I the woman, but something must be done for the cause of virtue.

Townsman. But one would think this were a common crime, and required the rigorous effects of the law to stay its progress. I in truth have more faith in woman, and as to the law, I'd rather quietly ship her back to England, than thus crush her by such an exposure.

Rawson. You are right, besides it is a sin better known to itself than to the public. 'Tis strange who the father is.—But let us to the market-place and see how poor Hester stands her hard fate. Exeunt. L. H. 1st E.

SCENE SECOND. THE MARKET-PLACE.

An old-fashioned Boston street. In the C of the Stage a platform four feet high. Steps in front. A rail around the top of platform. The structure represents the Pillory. On R. from 2d to 4th. E. a building representing a City Hall, with a stoop across the front two steps high, and broad enough for Characters to stand upon. Balcony, with columns to support it. Hester is discovered on the Pillory, with her child in her arms. The Beadle stands at foot of Steps, L. Two Soldiers R. & L. of steps. Four Soldiers with their halberts, behind the Governor's chair on the stoop. Citizens on the left from 2d to 4th E. Wilson and Dimmesdale on the Stoop. Chillingworth, Townsman, Swamp-fox, and Rawson above 1st E. L. H. Gossip, Small, Mercy and Child, in front of Crowd L. Hibbins disguised as a witch L. between 2d and 3d E.

Chillingworth. I pray you, good Sir, who is this woman? and wherefore is she here set up to public shame?

Townsman. You must needs be a stranger in this region, friend, else you would surely have heard of Mistress Hester Prynne and her evil doings. She hath raised a great scandal in godly Master Dimmesdale's church. The sight is a pity.

Chillingworth. Indeed! (Chillingworth turns and looks for a moment at Hester. Hester observes Chillingworth, and starts. Chillingworth motions her to be silent by placing his fingers on his lips.

You say truly, it is a pity. But who will hear the cause?

Townsman. The Governor, for whom they wait, and other magistrates.

Chillingworth. And what may be their office, now seated upon the porch yonder?

Townsman. The older of the two, and at the right, is the celebrated Reverend Mr. Wilson. The young man with pale face, is the Reverend Master Dimmesdale, of great eloquence, and stands very high with the godly people of Boston.

Chillingworth. Pray tell me more of this. I am a stranger, and have been a wanderer sorely against my will. I have met with grievous mishaps by sea and land, and have been long held in bonds among the heathen folk, to the southward, and am now brought hither by this Indian, to be redeemed out of my captivity. Will it please you, therefore, to tell me of Hester Prynne's offences? and what has brought her to yonder scaffold?

Townsman. Truly, friend; it must gladden your heart, after your sojourn in the wilderness, to find yourself at length in a land where iniquity is searched out, and punished, as here in godly New-England. Yonder woman, sir, you must know, was the wife of a certain learned man, English by birth, but who had long dwelt in Amsterdam whence some good time agone, he was minded to cross over and cast his lot with us of the Massachusetts. To this purpose he sent his wife before him, remaining himself to look after some necessary affairs. Marry, good sir, in some two years or less, that the woman has been a dweller here in Boston, no tidings having come of this learned gentleman, and his young wife, left to her own misguidance, is thus exposed and branded with the letter A, which stands for adultery.

Chillingworth. Ah! Aha!—I understand.—So learned a man as you speak of, should have learned this, too, in his books. And who, by your favor, sir, may be the father of yonder babe?—It is some two or three months old, I should judge.

Townsman. Of a truth, friend, that matter remaineth a

riddle; and the Daniel who shall expound it, is yet a-wanting. Madam Hester absolutely refuseth to speak to that point, and the magistrates laid their heads together in vain to find that out; peradventure the guilty one stands looking on at this sad spectacle unknown of man, and forgetting that God sees him.

Chillingworth. The learned man should come himself, to look into the mystery.

Townsman. It behoves him well, if he be still in life. Now, my good sir, our Massachusetts magistracy, bethinking themselves, that this woman is youthful and fair, and doubtless was strongly tempted to her fall;—and that, moreover, as is most likely, her husband may be at the bottom of the sea;—they have not been bold enough to put in force the extremity of the law against her. The penalty thereof is death, but in their tenderness of heart, they doomed Mistress Prynne to stand a space of three hours on yonder platform; and then, for the remainder of her natural life, to wear the mark of shame upon her bosom.

Chillingworth. Thus she will be a living sermon against her sin, and then mayhap, for an epitaph, the ignominious letter will be engraved upon her tombstone. (Enter Governor C. D.) But stay, that is the Governor, I take it. Let us stand aside, and see what may be the result. As Governor Bellingham steps foward on the porch, there is a stir among the crowd.

Governor. Hearken unto me, Hester Prynne. As the chief magistrate of this state, I am performing a duty more sad than any other that could befall me. Here, in the market-place, before the whole town's people, you stand—a public mark for the finger of shame to point at. It is not my purpose to torment you by dwelling at length upon the nature of your sin. I believe there is a mitigant, a balm for you, in revealing the name of him linked with yours in this misdeed. May Heaven give you strength to the performance of this duty, which you owe yourself and the public. Speak! (a pause, Hester keeps silent.) She answers not. (to Wilson. Governor sits down.)

Wilson. (rises) Hester Prynne, I have striven with my

young brother here, under whose preaching of the word you have been privileged to sit. I have sought, I say, to persuade this godly youth, that he should deal with you here in the face of Heaven. Knowing your natural temper better than I, he could the better judge what arguments to use, whether of tenderness or sorrow, such as might prevail over your obstinacy; insomuch that you should no longer hide the name of him who tempted you to this grievous fall. But he opposes me, urging that it were wronging the very nature of woman to force her to lay open her hearts' secrets in such broad daylight, and in presence of so great a multitude. What say you to it, once again, brother Dimmesdale! Must it be thou or I that shall deal with this poor sinner's soul?

Bellingham. Good master Dimmesdale, the responsibility of this woman's soul lies greatly with you. It behoves you, therefore, to exhort her to repentance, and to confession as a proof and consequence thereof.

Wilson. Speak to the woman, my brother. It is of moment to her soul, and therefore, as the worshipful Governor says, momentous to thine own, in whose charge hers is. Exhort her to confess the truth!

Dimmesdale. (rises slowly with his hand on his heart.) Hester Prynne, thou hearest what this good man says, and seest the accountability under which I labor. If thou feelest it to be for thy soul's peace, and that thy earthly punishment will thereby be made more effectual to salvation, I charge thee, speak out the name of thy fellow-sinner. Be not silent from any mistaken pity and tenderness for him; for, believe me, Hester, though he were to step down from a high place, and stand there beside thee on thy pedestal of shame, yet better were it so, than to hide a guilty heart through life. What can thy silence do for him, except it tempt him—yea, compel him, as it were—to add hypocrisy to sin? Heaven hath granted thee an open ignominy, that thereby thou mayest work out an open triumph over the evil within thee, and the sorrow without. Take heed how thou deniest to him—who, perchance, hath not the courage to grasp for himself—that bitter but wholesome cup that is now presented to thy lips.   Hester Prynne, speak out the guilty name!

(Hester shakes her head, indicating No! after which Dimmesdale sits.)

Wilson. (Rises.) Woman, transgress not beyond the limits of Heaven's mercy! That little babe hath been gifted with a voice, to second and confirm the counsel which thou hast heard.   Speak out the name! that thy repentance may avail to take the Scarlet Letter off thy breast.   (A pause.)

Hester. (looking into the troubled eyes of Dimmesdale.) Never! It is too deeply branded. Ye cannot take it off, and would that I might endure *his* agony, as well as mine! never!

Chillingworth. (in the crowd.) Speak, woman! speak! and give thy child a father!

Hester. I will not speak! and my child must seek a heavenly Father; she shall never know an earthly one!

Dimmesdale. (aside.) She will not speak—wondrous strength and generosity of a woman's heart!—she will not speak!

Bellingham. Good people of Boston, all has been done that can be done to exhort this woman to name the companion of her guilt.   She has stood the terrible trial as one hardened, and may that God who tempers all things to righteousness, temper her disposition to divulge the name of him who has helped her to fasten this misdeed on our fair town. Hester Prynne, I leave you to your own conscience! (Exit all from the porch through the door.   The Beadle motions to Hester to leave the platform, two Soldiers follow the Beadle, Hester next, two Soldiers follow.   The people fall in behind and form procession.   They march down centre and exit 1st E. L. H.   As Hester turns to L. Mistress Hibbins speaks to her.)

Hibbins. You stand it bravely, Hester.   A stout heart has Hester Prynne. (aside.)   Hibbins immediately comes over and hides behind a column of the City Hall and watches Townsman and Chillingworth.

Chillingworth. It irks me much she did not tell his name, that we might know at least that much of the partner of her iniquity.   But he will be known!

Townsman. In truth, I doubt it, unless he comes foward himself.—Evident he was not here in the crowd, and if he were, a baser coward never walked God's earth, to stand silent and see her suffer thus.

Chillingworth. To me that's a mystery, and he still dwells here in Boston. And what disposition do they make of her now?

Townsman. Back to the prison, and when to-morrow comes, or perhaps a later day, they will thrust her forth to meet and battle with the world as best she can.

Chillingworth. Disgraced and homeless! Pointed at, perhaps a beggar! a wanderer! a letter of shame blazing upon her bosom, and a babe buckled upon her back. But he shall be known. He shall be known. *He shall be known.*

Exit Chillingworth, Townsman and Indian, L. F. E.

SCENE THIRD.

Same as the first, under moonlight-effects. A light seen in the Prison window. Hibbins enters quickly from L. H. F. E.

Hibbins. I'll watch and learn more. A fine story this for witchcraft, if I but get at the root of it, and may be, Mistress Hester, I'll find out your partner without the telling of your mouth; but stay! they come, and the shadow of this tree shall have ears, and hear words for the tongue's prattle. (Retires behind stump of tree R. H. F. E.)

Enter Chillingworth and Townsman, (L. 1st E.)

Chillingworth. Yes, I have satisfied my Indian companion, who has gone for the night to dwell with some of his kind, who hold a small camp hard by. On the morning I shall arrange my ransom with the Governor.

Townsman. And I hope all things will be to your liking. There' is the prison, that contains the branded Hester, and she must, as I take it, now sleep soundly after her exposure. (Brackett enters from prison-door with lantern in hand.) Here comes the jailor! I'll speak to him, and tell him that the Governor sends you for a night's shelter. A fair night, Master Brackett! The moon will be your better lantern, or you have far to go.

Brackett. I, marry! And is it you, Master Townsman?

Townsman. Ever the same. The Governor sends this stranger, one Chillingworth, to rest with you to-night. You will care for him as best you can.

Brackett. Our best is but ill, but ill betide me if I fail to do my best. I'll take thee in ere I depart, for I must hasten to find a medicine-man. Mistress Hester wanders in her mind, and I wonder not at it. I bethought me she was over-brave and stout of heart, and would pass through this day without a blanch or ache.

Chillingworth. Then, good Master Brackett, go no further; put by thy lantern, and save thy walk. Physical science has been my study. It would please me to tend to Hester's wants,—may I serve you?

Brackett. I, faith, and on the instant, for, I fear me, she will do some half-frenzied mischief to the poor babe, as well as to herself.

Chillingworth. Fear nothing, my medicines are potent.

Brackett. An' your worship can accomplish her health, I shall own thee for a man of skill indeed. She is like a possessed one, and there lacks little I should take in hand, and drive Satan out of her with stripes.

Chillingworth. Think not of that. Master Townsman, thanks for your attendance here, and to-morrow we will meet again. Good-night.

Townsman. Good-night, and an undisturbed rest. (Exit L. 1st E.)

Brackett. A sorry place—a prison to lodge in, but better than no place at all, and not a prisoner. (Brackett and Chillingworth enter prison.)

Hibbins. (Advances from tree to centre.) Roger Chillingworth! Hester ill! and it were strange, were she not so. This strange interest grows apace. Chillingworth! a new name for godly Boston, and I ne'er heard it before. I too will enter and offer comfort to Hester. (She stands in shade of the tree, drops off her over-skirt, takes her shawl off her head, and removes false hair, and in an instant appears the well-dressed Mistress Hibbins, the sister of Governor Bellingham. After taking off her disguise, she ties them up in a colored handkerchief.) It is the way of witchcraft to learn by stealth. (Ascends steps and knocks twice at door.)

Brackett. (Comes to door.) Why, good Mistress Hibbins! and at this time of night!

Hibbins. Yes, Master Brackett, I come to inquire about

the sick prisoner, and how Hester stood her exposure to-day.

Brackett. You shall know both. Come in. (Exeunt.)

SCENE FOURTH.

Interior of Prison (in 3) representing a whitewashed room (Boxed) L. H. 2d E; a heavy oaken door with cross-bars above its centre. R. H. 1st E; a window. Against flat L. C; a low wooden bedstead neatly fixed, and Hester's babe upon it. At R. C. a table covered with white ruffled drapery; a stone pitcher, tin cup and candle lighted on table; two stools. Hester discovered sitting R. of table, hair in a disordered state, hanging over her shoulders, with the moonlight falling across her head and shoulders through the window. Chillingworth standing L. of table.

Chillingworth. My old studies in alchemy, and my sojourn for more than a year among a people well versed in the kindly properties of simples, have made a better physician of me than many that claim the medicine degree. (Drops medicine in a tin cup from a small bottle taken from his breast-pocket.) Now, woman, since your child,—I said yours, not mine! has found ease from my drug, let it administer to yours. (Offers the cup to Hester who refuses to take it, at the same time gazing with marked apprehension into his face.) Foolish woman, why should I harm thee, or thy misgotten babe? The medicine is potent for good, and, were it my child, yea, mine own, as well as thine! I could do no better for it, or thee. I know not Lethe or Nepenthe, but I have learned many new secrets in the wilderness, and here is one of them—a recipe that an Indian taught me, in requital for some of mine own, that were as old as Paracelsus. Drink it! It may be less soothing than a sinless conscience. That I cannot give thee, but it will calm the swell and heaving of thy passion, like oil thrown on the waves of a tempestuous sea. Drink it! (Offers to Hester. She receives it with a look of doubt.)

Hester. I have thought of death, have wished for it, would e'en have prayed for it, were it fit that such as I should pray for anything. Yet if death be in this cup, I bid thee think again, ere thou beholdest me quaff it.   See! It is even now at my lips.

Chillingworth. Drink then:—dost thou know me so little, Hester Prynne?   Are my purposes wont to be so shallow? Even if I imagine a scheme of vengeance, what could I do better for my object than to let thee live?—than to give thee medicines against all harm and peril of life;—so that this burning shame may still blaze upon thy bosom? (lays his finger on the Scarlet Letter.   Hester shrinks.)   Live, therefore, and bear about thy doom with thee, in the eyes of men and women,--in the eyes of him thou didst call thy husband,—in the eyes of yonder child!   And that thou mayest live, take off this draught. (Hester drains the cup, lets it fall upon the floor, and sinks back into the chair.   Chillingworth brings the old chair from beside the bed and sits opposite to Hester.)   Hester, I ask not wherefore nor how thou hast fallen into the pit, or, say rather, thou hast ascended to the pedestal of infamy, on which I found thee.   The reason is not far to seek.   It was my folly, and thy weakness.   I—a man of thought,—the book-worm of great libraries,—a man already in decay, having given my best years to feed the hungry dreams of knowledge,—what had I to do with youth and beauty like thine own!   Mis-shapen from my birth-hour, how could I delude myself with the idea that intellectual gifts might veil physical deformity in a young girl's fancy!   Men call me wise.   If sages were ever wise in their own behoof, I might have foreseen all this.   I might have known that, as I came out of the vast and dismal forest, and entered this settlement of christian men, the very first object to meet my eyes would be thyself, Hester Prynne, standing up, a statue of ignominy before the people.   Nay, from the moment we came down the old church steps together, a married pair, I might have beheld the bale-fire of that Scarlet Letter blazing at the end of our path!

Hester. Thou knowest that I was frank with thee.   I felt no love, nor feigned any.

Chillingworth. True.   It was my folly!   I have said it, I had lived in vain.   The world had been so cheerless!   My heart was a habitation large enough for many guests, but lonely and chill, without a household fire. I longed to kindle one. It seemed not so wild a dream. Old as I was, and sombre as I was, and mis-shapen as I was,—that the simple bliss, which is scattered far and wide, for all mankind to gather up, might yet be mine. And so, Hester, I drew thee into my heart, into its innermost chamber, and sought to warm thee by the warmth thy presence made there!

Hester. I have greatly wronged thee.

Chillingworth. We have wronged each other; mine was the first wrong, when I betrayed thy budding youth into a false and unnatural relation with my decay. Therefore, as a man who has not thought and philosophized in vain, I seek no vengeance, plot no evil against thee. Between thee and me, the scale hangs fairly balanced. Hester, the man lives who has wronged us both ! Who is he?

Hester. (Starts and looks him in the face.) Ask me not. My heart is barred and bolted. My tongue is clinched. Thou shalt never know !

Chillingworth. Never, sayest thou? Never know him ? Believe me, Hester, there are few things,—either in the outward world, or, to a certain depth, in the invisible sphere of thought,—few things hidden from the man who devotes himself earnestly and unreservedly to the solution of a mystery. Thou mayest cover up thy secret from the prying multitude; thou mayest conceal it, too, from the ministers and magistrates, even as thou didst this day, when they sought to wrench the name out of thy heart, and give thee a partner on thy pedestal. But as for me, I come to the inquest with other senses than they possess. I shall seek this man, as I have sought truth in books; as I have sought gold in alchemy. There is a sympathy that will make me conscious of him. I shall see him tremble. I shall feel myself shudder suddenly and unawares. Sooner or later he must needs be mine ! (Hester shudders and clasps her hand over her heart.)

Hester. (aside.) My God ! what power this man's words have over me ! I feel as if he had unbarred my heart, and reads his name, in letters of blazing fire. Oh Heaven! make me speechless rather than let me tell it!

Chillingworth. Thou wilt not reveal his name? Not the less is he mine. He bears no letter of infamy wrought into his garments, as thou dost; but I shall read it on his heart. Yet fear not for him! Think not I shall interfere with Heaven's own method of retribution, or, to my own loss, betray him to the gripe of human law. Neither imagine that I shall contrive aught against his life; No, nor against his fame, if, as I judge, he be a man of fair repute. Let him live! Let him hide himself in outward honor, if he may! Not the less he shall be mine!

Hester. Thy acts are like mercy, but thy words interpret thee as a terror.

Chillingworth. One thing, thou that wast my wife, I would enjoin upon thee. Thou hast kept the secret of thy paramour, keep likewise mine! There are none in this land that know me. Breathe not to any human soul that thou didst ever call me husband! Here, on this wild outskirt of the earth, I shall pitch my tent; for elsewhere a wanderer, and isolated from human interest, I find here a woman, a man, a child, between whom and myself there exist the closest ligaments. No matter whether of love or hate; no matter whether of right or wrong! Thou and thine, Hester Prynne, belonging to me, my home is where thou art and where he is. But betray me not!

Hester. Wherefore dost thou desire it? Why not announce thyself openly, and cast me off at once?

Chillingworth. It may be because I will not encounter the dishonor that besmirches the husband of a faithless woman. It may be for other reasons. Enough; it is my purpose to live and die unknown. Let, therefore, thy husband be to the world as one already dead, and of whom no tidings shall ever come. Recognize me not, by word, by sign, by look. Breathe not the secret, above all, to the man thou wottest of. Shouldst thou fail me in this, beware! His fame, his position, his life, will be in my hands. Beware!

Hester. I will keep thy secret, as I keep his.

Chillingworth. Swear it! (with a smile.)

Hester. Why dost thou smile at me? Art thou like the black man that haunts the forest round about us? Hast thou enticed me into a bond that will prove the ruin of my soul!

Chillingworth. Not thy soul, no, not thine. Hester Prynne, swear to keep my secret?

Hester. I have said I will keep thy secret as I have his.

Chillingworth. Swear it! (Points Hester to kneel. She falls on her knees beside the table.)

Hester. I swear! (crossing her hands upon the Scarlet Letter.)

PICTURE, curtain falls to slow music.

END ACT FIRST.

ACT II.

Scene First. (In two.)

A LAPSE OF SEVEN YEARS.

The library and study of Dimmesdale and Chillingworth. The room represents an old-fashioned, wainscoted apartment. Several book-cases painted on the scene. R. C. table, with several books on it, pen, ink, paper, &c., &c. At L. second E, a large, open window through which are seen the tops of the village houses and a white church-steeple, illuminated by the warm rays of the setting sun. Immediately in front of the window is a large table with chemical apparatus. Dimmesdale is discovered sleeping in a chair L. of table. Dimmesdale is much changed, looking pale and thin, the bosom of his dress is partly open. Chillingworth is also much changed, more bent in form. His hair has become white. His face is deeply marked with the lines of melancholy, and indications of a student.

Chillingworth. (Enters L. 1st E. with an arm-full of herbs and large leaves. He lays them upon the table at window. He discovers Dimmesdale sleeping, passes behind table R. C. leans over and looks into the open dress of Dimmesdale.)

Chillingworth. Sleeping,—So, So!—wrought into the very flesh, and over his heart—Hush! (passes carefully over to L. 1st E. and exit. Dimmesdale awakens in time to see Chillingworth, starts and hastily fixes his dress.)

Dimmesdale. Chillingworth! what a strange man is this, of deep thoughts, and great knowledge, and though companionable to me in such things, yet otherwise how I shrink from him, and fear the scrutiny of his weird eyes that seem to know my very soul. To me he seems like a memory of a frightful dream, that constantly haunts, but realizes nothing. I like and dislike him, both at once. Now three years and more since he was made resident here with me, by my godly friends, to look after my health; but he looks in vain for the source of my ailment, and needs must burrow to the centre of the earth, or gather his herbs from another planet, ere he will find my nepenthe or my secret—but, stay, he comes again. (Enter Chil-

lingworth with more herbs, and places them on the table at the window.)
Where, my kind doctor Chillingworth, didst thou gather
those herbs with such dark and flabby leaves?

Chillingworth. (at window.) Even in the grave-yard here at
hand. They are new to me. I found them growing out
of a grave which bore no tomb-stone, nor other memorial
of the dead, save these ugly weeds that have taken upon
themselves to keep whoever it may be in remembrance.

They grew out of his or her heart, to typify, it may be,
some hideous secret that was buried with him or her,
which they had done better to confess during life.

Dimmesdale. Perhaps they earnestly desired it, but could
not.

Chillingworth. And wherefore not, since all the powers of
nature call so earnestly for the confession of sin, that these
black leaves have sprung up out of a buried heart, to make
manifest an unspoken crime.

Dimmesdale. That, good sir, is but a fantasy of yours.
There can be, if I forbode aught, no power, short of the
Divine mercy, to reveal, whether by words, by type, or em-
blem, the secrets that may be buried with a human heart.
The heart making itself guilty of such secrets, must per-
force hold them until the day when all hidden things shall
be disclosed. And I conceive, moreover, that the heart
holding such miserable secrets as you speak of, will yield
them up at that last day, not with reluctance, but with a
joy unutterable.

Chillingworth. Then why not reveal them here? Why
should not the guilty ones sooner avail themselves of this
unutterable joy?

Dimmesdale. They mostly do. (placing his hand over his heart.)
Many, many a poor soul hath given its confidence to me,
not only on their death-bed, but while strong in life. Oh!
what a relief have I witnessed in those sinful brethren!

Chillingworth. Yes, and why should a wretched man,
guilty, we will say, of murder, prefer to keep the corpse
buried in his own heart rather than fling it forth at once,
and let the universe take care of it? And yet *some men*
bury their secrets thus.

Dimmesdale. True, there are such men. It may be they
are kept silent by the very constitution of their nature;
they shrink from displaying themselves blackened in view
of men; because thence-forward, no good can be achieved
by them; no evil of the past can be redeemed by better
service. So, to their own unutterable torment, they go
about among their fellow-creatures, looking pure as new-
fallen snow; while their hearts are all speckled and spot-
ted with iniquity of which they cannot rid themselves.

Chillingworth. They deceive themselves, they fear to take
up the shame that rightfully belongs to them. Their regard of man, their zeal for God's service, their holy im-
pulses may or may not co-exist in their hearts with the
evil inmates to which their guilt has unbarred the door,
and which must needs propagate a hellish breed within
them. But if they seek to glorify God, let them not lift
heaven-ward their unclean hands! If they would serve
their fellow-men, let them do it by making manifest the
power and reality of conscience, in constraining them to
penitential self-abasement. Would you have me to believe,
O wise and pious friend, that a false show can be better—
can be more for God's glory, or man's welfare, than God's
own truth? Trust me, such men deceive themselves?

Dimmesdale. It may be so.—But now, I would ask my
well-skilled physician, whether in good sooth, he deems
me to have profited by his kindly care of this weak frame
of mine? (The clear wild laugh of Pearl is heard without. Chillingworth looks out of the window.)

Chillingworth. There is no law, nor reverence for authority, nor regard for human ordinances, or opinions, right
or wrong, mixed up in that child's composition. There
she is, dancing upon a grave. I saw her the other day,
bespatter the Governor himself with water, at the cattle-
trough in Spring lane. What in Heaven's name is she?
Is the imp altogether evil? Hath she affections? Hath
she any discoverable principle of being?

Dimmesdale. None,—save the freedom of a broken law.
Whether capable of good, I know not.

Chillingworth. There goes a woman, who, be her demerits

what they may, hath none of that mystery of hidden sinfulness which we deem so grievous to be borne. Is Hester Prynne the more miserable, think you, for that Scarlet letter on her breast?

Dimmesdale. I do verily believe it. (Places his hand over his heart.) Nevertheless, I cannot answer for her. But still, methinks, it must needs be better for the sufferer to be free to show his pain, as this poor woman, than to cover it all up in his heart.

Chillingworth. They, the magistrates, and the godly men of our good city, talk of taking Hester's child from her. They purport that she is not fit to bring her up in the path she should go. Will you hear the case to-morrow? And if so, will it please you, that I go with you?

Dimmesdale. (Restless.) With all my heart. I have been sent for in consultation.

Chillingworth. You inquired of me, a little time agone, my judgment touching your health.

Dimmesdale. I did, and would gladly learn it. Speak frankly, I pray you, be it for life or death.

Chillingworth. Plainly then, the disorder is a strange one, so far at least, as the symptoms have been laid open to my observations. Looking daily at you, good sir, and watching the tokens of your aspect, now for months gone by, I deem you a man sore sick,—it may be, yet not so sick but that an *instructed* and watchful physician might have hope to cure you. But I know not what to say—the disease is what I seem to know, yet know it not.

Dimmesdale. You speak in riddles, learned sir.

Chillingworth. Then to speak more plainly, and I crave pardon, sir. for this needful plainness of my speech. Let me ask,—as your friend,—as one having charge, under Providence, of your life and physical well-being, have all the operations of this disorder been fairly laid open and recounted to me?

Dimmesdale. How can you question it? Surely it were child's play to call in a physician, and then hide the sore!

Chillingworth. You would tell me, then, that I know all? (fixing his eyes intesely on him.) Be it so! But again! a bod-

ily disease, which we may look upon as whole and entire
within itself, may, after all, be but a symptom of some ailment in the spiritual part.   Your pardon, once again, good
sir, of all men whom I have known, you, sir, are he whose
body is closest conjoined and imbued and identified, so to
speak, with the spirit whereof it is the instrument.

Dimmesdale. Then I need ask no further.   You deal not,
I take it, in medicine for the soul!

Chillingworth. (Looking him full in the face.) Thus a sickness,—a sore place,—if we may so call it,—in your spirit,
hath immediately its appropriate manifestations in your
bodily frame.   Would you therefore, that your physician
heal the bodily evil?   How may this be, unless you first
lay open to him the trouble of your soul?

Dimmesdale (Passionately.) No! not to thee!   Not to an
earthly physician!   But if it be the soul's disease, then do
I commit myself to the one physician of the soul!   He, if
it stand with his good pleasure, can cure, or he can kill!
Let him do with me as in his justice and wisdom he shall
see fit.   But who art thou (standing up at table.) that med-
dlest in this matter?   That darest thrust thyself between
the sufferer and his God? (Rushes off R. 1st E.)

Chillingworth. (quietly looking after him.) It is well to have
made this step. (Smiles.)   There is nothing lost: we shall be
friends anon.   But see, now, how passion takes hold of this
man, and hurrieth him out of himself!   As with one passion, so with another!   He hath done a wild thing ere now,
this pious Master Dimmesdale, in the hot passions of his
heart!   A rare case!   I must needs look deeper into it.
Were it only for the art's sake, I will search this matter to
the bottom.   Now for the mysteries of this day's collection.
(Goes to table at window and looks over the herbs and leaves.) These
herbs have nothing to conceal; their nature yields readily
to the chemist's power, and all of good or bad can be ex-
tracted for truth's sake.   If some men's hearts could be as
easily looked into, what frightful revelations would be
given to the world! (Close in.)

SCENE SECOND.   (In five.)

The scene represents a cove or inlet in Boston harbor.   The back-ground
   shows the sea-shore with waves in gentle motion, washing up upon
   the stage.   A light, sunny sky.   Time, afternoon.   On the R. H.
   rocks and trees; on the L. from 2 to 4 E., a small white cottage with
   a porch along its front, posts and overhanging shed, richly clustered
   with wild vines and flowers.   An old-fashioned rocking chair on
   the porch.   A toy cradle and a small chair on the ground in front
   of the porch.   Hester and Pearl enter from cottage down the steps.

Hester. Now, my darling Pearl, you have learned well
your lessons, and for this you shall have a nice play among
the shells and sea-birds upon the sands in the sunlight of
this beautiful day.—But, my darling, keep away from those
rocks yonder; the water is very deep there, and should
you fall in, I would lose my little Pearl forever.

Pearl. (goes to the margin of the water.) O mamma! look at
this beautiful shell!—but yonder is a better place.   Come,
come into the pool with me! (Runs off R. H. 4th E.)

Hester. Ah! dear child, all things are beautiful to you
now.   Trouble has not yet clouded your sunshine.   But
the storms of life await us all. (Comes down to C. opposite to
Second Entrance, looks off L.)   An my eyes deceive me not,
that crooked and bending form, pulling up weeds and roots,
is Roger Chillingworth.   How changed he is!   Dare I
but speak to him!—he comes this way.   Dare I but speak
my mind! (Retires and leans against the porch.   Chillingworth enters, looking around for plants, stoops to pull some leaves at R. 2d E.
Hester comes to C.)   Roger Chillingworth, I would speak a
word with you—a word that concerns us much.

Chillingworth. Aha! and is it Mistress Hester that has
a word for old Roger Chillingworth?—with all my heart.
(Gets up and comes to C.)   Why Mistress, I hear good tidings
of you on all hands.   Great stories are told of your watching and nursing of the poor and the sick, and no longer
ago than yester-eve, a magistrate, a wise and godly man,
was discoursing of your affairs, and whispered me that
there had been question concerning you in the council.
It was debated whether or no, with safety to the common

weal, yonder Scarlet Letter might be taken off your bosom. On my life, Hester, I made my entreaty to the worshipful magistrates that it might be done forthwith.

Hester. (After a pause.) It lies not in the pleasure of the magistrates to take off this badge. Were I worthy to be quit of it, it would fade away of its own nature, or be transformed into something that should speak a different purport.

Chillingworth. Nay, then, wear it, if it suit you better. A woman must needs follow her own fancy touching the adornment of her own person. The letter is gayly embroided, and shows right bravely on your bosom! (Hester looks steadily at Chillingworth during this speech.) What see you in my face, that you look at it so earnestly?

Hester. Something that would make me weep, if there were any tears bitter enough for it. But let it pass! (Points off L. 1st E, where Dimmesdale is supposed to be standing.) It is of yonder miserable man that I would speak—Master Dimmesdale,—who stands there, and has been walking with you.

Chillingworth. And what of him? Not to hide the truth, Mistress Hester, my thoughts just now happen to be busy with the gentleman, so speak freely, and I will make answer.

Hester. When we last spake together, now seven years agone, it was your pleasure to extort a promise of secrecy as touching the further relations betwixt yourself and me. As the life and good fame of yonder man were in your hands, there seemed no choice to me, save to be silent in accordance with your behest, yet it was not without heavy misgivings that I thus bound myself for having cast off all duty towards all other human beings. There remained a duty toward him; and something whispered me that I was betraying it, in pledging myself to keep your counsel. Since that day no man is so near to him as you. You tread behind his every footstep, you are beside him sleeping and waking, you dwell under the same roof with him, you search his thoughts, you burrow and rankle in his heart! your clutch is on his life, and you cause him to die daily a living death, and still he knows you not!—In permitting this, I have surely acted a false part by the only man to whom the power was left me to be true!

Chillingworth. What choice had you? My finger pointed at this man, would have hurled him from his pulpit into a dungeon,—thence peradventure to the gallows!

Hester. It had been better so!

Chillingworth. What evil have I done the man? I tell thee, Hester Prynne, the richest fee physician ever earned from monarch, could not have bought such a care, as I have wasted on this miserable priest! But for my aid, his life would have burned away in torments within the first two years after the perpetration of *his* crime and *thine*, for, Hester, his spirit lacked the strength that could have borne up as *thine* has, beneath a burden like the Scarlet Letter. O, I could reveal a goodly secret! But enough! what art can do, I have exhausted on him. That he now breathes and creeps about on earth, is owing all to me!

Hester. Better that he had died at once!

Chillingworth. Yes, woman, thou sayest truly. Better he had died at once! Never did mortal suffer what this man has suffered, and all, all in the sight of his worst enemy! He knew that no friendly hand was pulling at his heart-strings, and that an eye was looking curiously into him which sought only evil, and found it. But he knew not that the eye and hand were mine! He fancied himself given over to a fiend, as a foretaste of what awaits him beyond the grave. Yes, indeed! he did not err! There was a fiend at his elbow!

Hester. Hast thou not tortured him enough? Has he not paid thee all?

Chillingworth. No! No! He has increased the debt. When I see myself as I was, and what I now am! Dost thou remember me, Hester, as I was seven years agone? And although I was in the autumn of my years, yet no life had been more peaceful and innocent than mine. Dost thou remember me? Was I not, though you might deem me cold, a man thoughtful for others, craving little for myself,—kind, true, just, and of constant, if not warm affection? Was I not all these?

Hester. All these, and more.

Chillingworth. And what am I now? A fiend! Who made me so? Who made me so?

Hester. (Shuddering,) It was myself! It was I, not less than he. Why hast thou not revenged thyself on me?

Chillingworth. I have left thee to the Scarlet Letter. If that hath not avenged me, I can do no more!

Hester. It has avenged thee!

Chillingworth. I judge no less, and now what wouldst thou with me touching this man?

Hester I must reveal the secret. (Firmly.) I must discover thee in thy true character. What may be the result I know not. But this long debt of confidence due from me to him, whose bane and ruin I have been, shall at length be paid. So far as concerns the overthrow or preservation of his fair fame and his earthly state. and perhaps his life, he is in thy hands; nor do I,—whom the Scarlet Letter has disciplined to truth, though it be the truth of red-hot iron, entering into the soul,—perceive advantage in his living any longer a life of ghastly emptiness. I shall not stoop to implore thy mercy. Do with him as thou wilt! There is no good for him,—no good for me,—no good for thee!—there is no good for little Pearl. There is no good to guide us out of this dismal maze!

Chillingworth. Woman, I could well nigh pity thee! Thou hast great elements.—Hadst thou met earlier with a better love than mine,—Did I say a better love than mine? No! No! a younger love than mine,—this evil had not been. I pity thee, for the good that hath been wasted in thy nature!

Hester. And I thee, for the hatred that has transformed a wise and a just man into a fiend. Wilt thou yet purge it out of thee, and be once more human? If not for his sake, then doubly for thine own, forgive, and leave his further punishment to the power that claims it! I said but now that there could be no good event for him, or thee, or me, who are here wandering together in a gloomy world of evil, and stumbling at every step, over the guilt wherewith we have strewn our paths. Is it not so? There might be good for thee alone, since thou hast been deeply wronged, and hast it at thy will to pardon. Wilt thou give up that only privilege? Wilt thou reject that price-less benefit?

Chillingworth. Peace, Hester, peace! It is not granted me to pardon. I have no such power as thou tellest me of. My old faith long forgotten comes back to me, and explains all that we do, and all that we suffer. By the first step awry, thou didst plant the germ of evil; but, since that moment, it has all been a dark necessity. Ye that have wronged me, are not sinful, save in a kind of typ-ical illusion; neither am I fiend-like, who has snatched a fiend's office. It is our fate. Let the black flower blossom as it may! Now go thy ways, and deal as thou wilt with yonder man, and I will go mine. (Betakes himself again to look-ing for herbs, pulls some large leaves from the side of a rock at R. 1st E. and exits. Hester contemplates him with wonderment.)

Hester. (Looking after him.) Was that man ever my hus-band? Is he the same that was?—Be it sin or not, I now hate thee! But O my God! what a change is wrought, what a contrast to those past days in that distant land of my birth when he used to emerge at eventide from the se-clusion of his study and sit down in the partial gloom of the day, and tell me he needed my smiles to extend the light and take the chill from around the scholar's heart. But, as now viewed through a dismal medium of a long past, I marvel that such scenes have been, and how I could have been wrought up to marry him.—It is my crime, that I even endured the lukewarm grasp of his hand, or suf-fered the smile of my lips and eyes to mingle with the weird and strange quality of his own. But what is my crime to his? My heart was young and the scholar's siren words captured my ear, and not my heart. He was full of years and wisdom, and betrayed me. But let the man be cautious who seeks to win the hand of a woman, unless he wins along with it the utmost love of her heart: with-out the love, it is but as the marble statue, the form without the warmth.—But this will not do, where's my little Pearl, (Retires up the stage and discovers Pearl off R. H. 3rd E.) There she stands, bedecking herself with sea-weeds, O my only bliss and burden! Pearl! Pearl! come hither child. (Hester comes down C. Pearl enters bedecked with sea-weeds, and the letter A, made of sea-greens, fixed upon her bosom.)

Pearl. I wonder if mother will ask me what this means. (Pearl stands in front of Hester, who observes the A on Pearl's bosom with astonishment.)

Hester. Why, Pearl, what have you got there?

Pearl. The great letter A.

Hester. But why dost thou wear it, child?

Pearl. Because you wear it. What does the Scarlet Letter mean, and why does the minister keep his hand over his heart?

Hester. O child, I wear it for the sake of the gold that is in the braid.

Pearl. But why does the minister keep his hand over his heart?

Hester. Hush, Pearl, hush!—Listen to the waves, singing on the beach. Come with me and I will tell you the sad story of the fairy and the deformed. (Exit into Cottage.)

SCENE THIRD.

A thick, wild forest in I. Enter L. 1st E, Mistress Hibbins, Swamp-lily, Spear-head, Fleet-wing and Weeping willow.

Hibbins. Now for a night of joy and wild revelations, and I speak not truth but ye shall see strange things. Come hither. (They all gather around at C. of stage.) As I wandered at midnight through the dark recesses of yonder gloomy and entangled wood where all fear the noxious bite of the snake, and the sharp teeth of the barking wolf, there alone, I encountered a four-legged thing with a human head and a tongue of fire that bade me do this work to-night. You, Lily of the Swamp, (To Indian girl bedecked with large swamp-lily leaves.) fly to those of your tribe that sport in the big waters and tell them to bring their offerings to the glen to-night, for when the yellow moon sits like a centre jewel in the crown of heaven, the big caldron must be made to dance by the hot fire of the blazing faggot. Tell them to bring the blue and the black fish, or one so small that it were caught in a pond no bigger than a thumb's nail. Away! Away! (Quit exit L. 1st E.) Spear-head! with all the sharpness of thy wits, hunt up thy little band that are out on the four-footed trail, and tell them not to fail to bring in the cunning fox! Its haunches are fine pulling for teeth like thine, and it feeds the wits.—(Exit R. 1st E.) And now, Fleet-wing, fly thou to thy craft, and tell them to bring in the wild pigeon, the robin, the blue-jay, the cat-bird or the soft-singing, golden-winged oriole. Away! Away! (Exit L. 1st E.) Weeping-willow! (To weeping-willow who is bedecked with twigs of willow.) Lay aside thy tears and for once forget your gallant lover who fell from the bow of the ship, and has the ocean for a great coffin. I say, forget thy lost lover. (Weeping-willow sighs.) A sigh, girl?— pshaw! There are other lovers to be found. I say, forget him, join in the mystic dance to-night; get thee gone, and find my Night-bird, send the trusty boy hither. I have a message for Hester Prynne, and thou shalt see to-night the Scarlet Letter reflecting from her bosom a weird light, like the moon on the sickly swamp.

Weeping-willow. Hester Prynne in the Glen!

Hibbins. Yes, Hester Prynne! Thou shalt see her in the glen to-night. Away! Away! (Exit R. 1st E.) And indeed, Hester Prynne, I can serve thee now. Too bitterly hast thou paid for the error of an unthinking moment. For seven long years has the finger of shame marked thee for its own. Roger Chillingworth, I'll cross thy path yet, and, Master Dimmesdale, thou shalt smile once more.-- (Whistle without.) Ah-ha! well does the whistle, made from the bone of the shrieking owl, tell me that my Night-bird comes. (Enter R. 1st E, Night-bird running, bedecked with black plumes.) And I greet thee with a cookey. (Takes a cake from her pocket, and gives it to Night-bird.) Come now, a cake pleas-ant to thy tooth, and made by Fairy fingers who took the sweet from the golden honey-suckle that grew in the even-ing star. Fly now, quick as thy black wings can carry thee to the white cottage by the beach, and put this into the hands of the Scarlet Letter. (Gives him a letter.) An thou wouldst have sport to-night, fail not to do as I bid thee, and bring her to the glen. (Night-bird starts to go. Calls him back.) Stay! Tell her, an she love Pearl, fail not to come! Away! Away! (Exit L. 1st E.) Now for the glen, and the wonders I shall work before my people by bringing the Scarlet Letter into their midst. (Exit R. 1st E.)

SCENE FOURTH.

A glen, full depth of the stage. Trees and wild vines overhanging embankments. The full moon is seen rising through the trees. In centre of the stage, a large caldron hanging from a tripod, with a blazing fire underneath. Groups of Indians and wild-looking white men and women, sitting around the stage, beating on Indian drums, &c. &c., while others are dancing around the caldron in time to their music. The whole scene making a grand and wild picture. The working of the moon is to pass up the back flat and disappear overhead so as to bring the calcium light effects upon Hester and the group at the end of the scene. After dancing three times around the caldron, they stop, an opening is made in front of the circle. Spear-head jumps up and drops the haunches of a fox in the caldron.

Spearhead. And this I bring, that's full of meat!
Hibbins. A fox, indeed, is rare and sweet!
Fleetwing. And I these birds, all fresh and clean!
Hibbins. The finest batch I have ever seen!
Swamp-lily. And I these fish, the black and the blue!
Hibbins. Indeed a prize, well done for you!
Blighted-trunk. And here are legs of toads and frogs,
          I caught but now in clumpy bogs!

(Dance around the caldron while singing chorus.)

Around, around the caldron fly,
While yet the moon fills yonder sky;
Stir well the soup;
Beat hard the drums;
We'll have our sport till morn-light comes.

Hibbins. (Sings.)

> O would I were the tempest-cloud,
> To sweep o'er earth with thunder loud ;
> I'd gather by night, I'd gather by day,
> The fruits in orchard, the fish in bay ;
> I'd gather the birds that floated high ;
> I'd pluck the stars from yonder sky,
> And here I'd bring the things you like,
> To feast with joy by day and night.

CHORUS.

> Around, around the caldron fly,
> While yet the moon fills yonder sky ;
> Stir well the soup ;
> Beat hard the drums ;
> We'll have our sport till morn-light comes.

(Night-bird whistles without, as if in the distance.)

Hibbins. Down, children, down! (They all stoop down and direct their attention to Hibbins.) Hear ye not the whistle of Night-bird! (Whistle again, nearer.) Be still as death. He brings one to our camp who has long been an outcast, and yet belongs not to our tribe. But ye shall hear me tell her such truths to-night as shall make her shake like the aspen, and look as pale as the will-o-the-wisp. We will yet count among our band the names of the Scarlet Letter and little Pearl. (A loud whistle.) Back and down! children, and move not until I speak! (They all retire up the stage, and lie down so as not to be discovered by Hester. Hibbins stands in C. of stage, leaning on her staff. Enter L. 1st E, Night-bird who runs to Hibbins, and points off L. 1st E. She beckons him to retire up the stage. Enter Hester with little Pearl.)

Hibbins. Aha! Mistress Hester, I am glad to see thee in the forest to-night. And, little Pearl, thou, too, art welcome. They say, child, thou art the lineage of the prince of the air. Wilt thou ride with me some fine night to see thy father? then thou shalt know wherefore the minister keeps his hand over his heart. (Hester starts.)

Hester. Woman, I know not what you say. What words have you for me?

Hibbins. (Aside to Hester.) Know not what I spake? It is

not for me to talk lightly of a learned and pious minister, like the Rev. Dimmesdale.

Hester. Thou knowest naught.

Hibbins. Fie, woman, fie! ha! ha! ha! ha! Dost thou think I have no memory. Thinks thou, I have forgotten the night of vigil, when one saintly man stood amid the glare of lightning, upon the platform in the market-place, and his wild laugh brought two others who stood there with him! I can tell a rose from a thistle even in the dark!—Hold down thy ear, and let me whisper a word. (She whispers in Hester's ear. Hester starts.)

Hester. Come, Pearl, come! let us fly from here.

Hibbins. Stay, Hester. It was not for these words I sent for thee. Look to little Pearl! The wolves of the law would take thy treasure from thee. Even now while yonder moon throws its silver rays across the door-way of Governor Bellingham, there sit in council men, who on the morrow will meet again to take from thee thy little Pearl. (Hester shrieks, falls upon her knees, and clasps Pearl.) Look to it, Hester Prynne. Be thou there, or Pearl is lost forever! Behold, my people, how much the Scarlet Letter feels the truth of your witch-queen!

PICTURE. They all rush forward at the word " Behold," and form a half circle about Hester, pointing at the Scarlet Letter on her bosom. The moon-light falls on Hester and Pearl. Hibbins and all, as the curtain descends, exclaim " The Scarlet Letter!"

End Second Act.

ACT III.

Scene First.

A large hall in the mansion of Governor Bellingham. Old portraits hanging on the wall. A table at R. 2d E, with helmet, breast-plate and sword on it. At R. C, a large table with books, pens, ink-stand, &c., &c. Bellingham discovered at head of the table, Dimmesdale R. of table, front, Chillingworth L. of table, front, Master Wilson R. of table, above Dimmesdale.

Bellingham. Were it not well that we take this child and place her under such instructions as would make her mother's fatal badge a terror? I admire not the way she adorns the child. I profess I have never seen the like since my days of vanity in old King James' time, when I was wont to esteem it a high favor to be admitted to a court-mask. There used to be a swarm of those small apparitions in holiday times, and we called them the children of the Lord of Mis-rule.

Wilson. Ah, indeed, what a little bird of scarlet plumage is she! Methinks I have seen just such figures when the sun has been shining on a richly-painted window, and throwing its brilliant rays across the figure of some beautiful child. It was but the other day I met this Pearl, as she is called, with her mother, and asked her name, to which the little prattler replied, that she was a rose her mother had plucked from the bush that grew beside the old prison door. This shows a wrong bringing up, and that she is a stranger to proper instructions. (Enter servant L. F. E.)

Servant. Your worship, one Hester Prynne would speak a word with you.

Bellingham. Admit her. (Exit servant.) She comes opportune. She is here, and with her little Pearl. (Enter Hester with Pearl L. F. E.) Hester Prynne, there has been much question concerning thee of late. The point hath been discussed whether we that are of authority, do well discharge our conscience by trusting an immortal soul, such as there is in yonder child, to the guidance of one who has stumbled amid the pit-falls of this world. Were it not wise, think you, that she be taken out of your charge, and instructed in the truths of heaven and earth?

Hester. (Standing with Pearl, L. C.) I teach my little Pearl what I have learned from this. (Laying her finger on Scarlet Letter.)

Bellingham. Woman, it is thy badge of shame. It is because of the stain, which that letter indicates, that we would transfer the child to other hands.

Hester. Nevertheless, this badge hath taught me,—it daily teaches me,—it teaches me at this moment,—lessons whereby my child may be the better and wiser.

Bellingham. We will look well at what we are about to do. Good master Wilson, what think you, hath this child such Christian nurture as befits one of her age?

Wilson. I fear not, unless the mother bestows as much care upon the child's moral instructions as she does upon her dress. I much fear you have not instructed the child in those heavenly truths which the human spirit at her tender years should be well imbued with. As you bend the twig, so the tree will grow. Dress the child in the garb of vanity, and you make a vain woman. Vanity loves flattery, by which many are fascinated from the ways of truth, and are lost to God. Hester, that child must be taken from your hands, and placed in those who will bring her up in the ways of righteousness!

(Pearl clings to her mother. Hester advances with firm step toward Wilson, and with great emotion looks him in the face.)

Hester. (After a pause.) God gave me this child! He gave her in requital of all things else which ye have taken from me. She is my happiness!—She is my torture, none the less. Pearl keeps me here in life! Pearl punishes me too! See ye not, she is the Scarlet Letter, only capable of being loved, and so endowed with a million-fold power of retribution for my sin?—God gave her to me, and ye shall not take her from me! I will die first!

Wilson. My poor woman, the child shall be well cared for!—far better than thou canst.

Hester. God gave her into my keeping! (Raising her voice

almost to a shriek.) I will not give her up! Speak thou for me! (Turning to Dimmesdale.) Speak thou for me. Thou wast my pastor, and hadst charge of my soul, and knowest me better than these men can. I will not lose my child! Speak for me! Thou knowest!—for thou hast sympathies which these men lack!—Thou knowest what is in my heart, and what are a mother's rights, and how much the stronger they are when that mother has but her child and the Scarlet Letter!—Look thou to it, I will not lose the child! Look to it! Without her love, I would be alone in this dark world; without this soul-treasure there would be nothing to keep my heart alive; my little sun-shine would be gone! In her I have indefeasible rights against the world, and in the sight of God, I will defend them! Look to it! Look to it! (She kneels and rapturously kisses Pearl.)

Dimmesdale. (Rises with emotion, and with his hand over his heart. Chillingworth intently watches the face of Dimmesdale all through the scene.) There is much truth in what she says. God gave her the child, and gave her, too, an instinctive knowledge of its nature and requirements, both seemingly so peculiar,—which no other mortal being can possess, and is there not a quality of awful sacredness in the relation between this mother and this child?

Bellingham. Ah! How is that, good Master Dimmesdale? Make that plain, I pray you!

Dimmesdale. It must be even so, for if we deem otherwise, do we not thereby say that the Heavenly Father hath lightly recognized a deed of sin, and made of no account the distinction between an unhallowed lust and a holy love? This child, of its father's guilt and its mother's shame, hath come from the hand of God, to work in many ways upon her heart, who pleads so earnestly and with such bitterness of spirit. The right to keep her was meant for the one blessing of her life! It was meant, doubtless, as the mother herself has told us, for a retribution too; a torture to be felt at many an unthought-of moment; a pang, a sting, an ever-recurring agony, in the midst of a troubled joy. Hath she not expressed the thought in the garb of the child, so forcibly reminding us of that red symbol which sears her bosom?

Wilson. Master Dimmesdale, I feared the mother had no better thought than to make a mountebank of the child!

Dimmesdale. (with eagerness.) O not so!—not so! She recognizes, believe me, the solemn miracle which God hath wrought, in the existence of that child,—and may she not feel, too, that this boon was meant above all things else, to keep the mother's soul alive, and to preserve her from other sin,—to remind her at every moment of her fall,—a sacred pledge, that, if she bring the child to heaven, the child also will bring its parent thither! Herein is the sinful mother far happier than the father. (Hester listens with marked attention.) For Hester's sake, let us leave them as Providence hath seen fit to place them. (Sits.)

Chillingworth. You speak, my friend, with a strange earnestness, and I must say with great truth as to the father.

Wilson. There is weighty import in what my young brother hath spoken. What say you, worshipful Master Bellingham? Had we not better let Hester take the child for the present? And with a watchful eye we can tell how the mother treasures her future.

Bellingham. I think so. He hath adduced such arguments, that we will even leave the matter as it now stands; so long, at least, as there shall be no further scandal in the woman. Thou canst depart, and with thee thy child,—but have a care, for should we observe, as she grows apace, a lack of any kind, she will stay no longer in thy custody. Go thy ways. (Hester stoops down and kisses Pearl. Pearl runs to the Governor, and kisses his hand. Exit Hester with Pearl L. F. E.) The little baggage hath witchcraft in her. I profess she needs no old woman's broom-stick to fly withal.

Chillingworth. A strange child! Would it be beyond a philosopher's research, think ye, gentlemen, to analyze that child's nature, and, from its make, find the mould, to give a shrewd guess as to who the father is?

Wilson. Nay; It would be sinful, in such a question, to follow the clue of profane philosophy, and still better, it may be, to leave the mystery as we find it.

Bellingham. And thereby every good Christian man hath a title to show a father's kindness toward the poor, deserted babe. (Governor rises.) Gentlemen, for awhile I have business of importance with Master Wilson. (Exit Governor and Wilson R. F. E.)

Chillingworth. Good Master Dimmesdale, you seem much moved in this woman's behalf.

Dimmesdale. Not more than I should in any woman so situated. (Rising.) But, my dear sir, I must depart to visit the apostle Eliot among his Indian converts. The day advances, and I must haste away ere it be too late. (Exit R. E. E. Chillingworth for a moment looks after him.)

Chillingworth. Ay, indeed! haste thee from a subject thou wilt not tarry with. But thou shalt be known! Thou shalt be known! (Exit R. F. E.)

(Hibbins comes from behind the drapery of one of the windows in flat, where she has been concealed during the whole scene. Her dress is that of Mistress Hibbins.)

Hibbins. So, So! Hester, I have done thee a service, and he has saved your child. Hester, I will have thee yet one of our tribe. Now to see what she thinks of the good work I have done! (Exit R. F. E.)

SCENE SECOND. (In one.)

A thick sapling-wood, running in perspective with a bit of land-scape to the right. Enter Hester with Pearl L. F. E.

Hester. This way, Pearl. We will wander a while in yonder thick and beautiful grove where so many wild flowers congregate to gladden my sad heart, and to please your young eyes. There, where I have so often sent my prayers to heaven, will I now lift my voice again to the great Father of mercy, who has this day saved for me my darling Pearl. To have lost thee, would have killed all the flowers, stayed the songs of the birds, the sweet whisperings of the brooks, and hung the heavens with a pall,— all would have been a suffocating void! God, I thank thee for my little Pearl! (Stoops to kiss Pearl, while so doing, Hibbins enters as the witch, L. F. E.   Stands leaning over Hester, with staff in hand.)

Hibbins. So, Hester, in tears of thankfulness! (Hester starts and looks up at Hibbins.) Fear not, 'tis only me, a better friend, too, than thou thinkest. Spoke I not the truth, and cautioned thee aright? Thy presence saved Pearl, and bravely didst thou stand up for thy own!

Hester. (Rises.) Indeed thou hast served me well, and my heart thanks thee for it. (Crosses to L. H.)

Hibbins. (Following her.) Hist! Hist! Wilt thou go with me to-night? There will be merry company in the forest, and I well-nigh promised the Black-man that comely Hester Prynne should make one of the merry group.

Hester. Make my excuse to him, so please you. I must tarry at home, and keep watch over my little Pearl. Had they taken her from me, I would willingly have gone with thee into the forest, and signed my name in the Black-man's book, and that, too, with mine own blood!

Hibbins. Ah! Hester, we shall have thee there anon! It is the only way to save thy jewel there. (Pointing to Pearl.) For those busy and ravenous wolves of the law will pester you to the last. Ay, in faith, they would save the child, as they call it, but kill the mother of a broken heart—ha! ha! ha! (Looking off left, sees Dimmesdale. Aside.) An my eyes deceive me not, that is Master Dimmesdale, returning from the Apostle Eliot. I would cross his path and whisper a word in his ear. Hester, you will yet be one of us, and thy little Pearl too. (Exit L.)

Hester. (Looking after her.) Dimmesdale! Oh! fate! if I could but stand in his way and speak a word with him! I will! This way, Pearl, this way! (Exit L.)

SCENE THIRD.   (In three.)

A beautiful wild grove.   Rock at R. C, for a seat, with bush and vines behind it,—a hiding-place for Chillingworth.   In centre of the stage, opposite to 3, a large tree, running up out of sight, convenient to conceal the form of Hibbins.   Chillingworth discovered plucking leaves and plants at rock R. C.

Chillingworth. Thus from day to day I seek companion-
ship, and my only pleasure, in plucking these strange plants
that abound hereabouts. I never dreamed of such a life
as this. I thought to have had another sphere than a wilderness for my old age to wander through. I thought to
have had a companion, and not to live so much alone, but
the unsearchable ways of God have interfered and de-
prived me of her whom my heart had singled out for comfort. It matters not how hard we may strive, or how sacred the object we desire to obtain, an inscrutable power
thrusts it aside, and we are forced to struggle in other directions, and for things we never thought of. But why
should I talk of this? There is and can be but one mission
now for me to struggle with; my beard has become gray
with it! my form is bent with it! He must be known.
He must be known! Who comes here? (Looking off L. 2d E.)
Hester and Pearl. (Turns to R. F. E. and sees Dimmesdale.)
And Dimmesdale! So, So! I will ensconce me here
awhile, and observe. (Gets behind the rock R. C. Enter Hester
and Pearl L. F. E.)

Hester There, go yonder, (Pointing off R. 2d E.) where
the sun is shining on that bit of beautiful meadow; gather
the wild flowers, and when I call you, come. (Exit Pearl R.
2d E.) He comes. (Stands a little up the stage C. Enter Dimmesdale L. H. F. E, crosses toward R. F.E.) Arthur Dimmesdale!
Arthur Dimmesdale!

Dimmesdale. (R. H.) Who speaks? (Hester comes down F.)
Hester Prynne, is it thou?

Hester. Even so, if I am in life, and if it be life as I have
lived these seven years!

Dimmesdale. Hast thou found no peace?

Hester. None! Hast thou?

Dimmesdale. Nothing but misery!   ·

Hester. Thou wrong'st thyself in this. Thou hast deeply repented. The people reverence thee, and surely thou
workest good among them! Doth this bring thee no
comfort?

Dimmesdale. More misery, Hester! Only the more misery! As concerns the good I may appear to do, I have

no faith in it. It must needs be a delusion. What can a
ruined soul like mine effect towards the redemption of
other souls? And as for the people's reverence, would
that it were turned to scorn and hatred! Canst thou deem
it a consolation, that I must stand up in my pulpit, and
meet so many eyes turned upward to my face, as if the
light of Heaven were beaming from it, and see my flock
listening to me as if a tongue of Pentecost were speaking?
I have laughed, in bitterness and agony of heart, at the
contrast of what I am! And Satan laughs at it!

Hester. Thou wrong'st thyself. Is there no reality in
the penitence thus sealed and witnessed by good works?

Dimmesdale. There is no substance in it! It is cold and
dead, and can do nothing for me! Of penance, I have
had enough! Of penitence, there has been none; else I
should long since have thrown off these garments of mock
holiness, and have shown myself to mankind as they will
see me at the judgment-seat. Happy are you, Hester
Prynne, that wear the Scarlet Letter openly upon your
bosom! Mine burns in secret! Thou little knowest what
a relief it is, after the torments of seven years' cheat, to
look into an eye that recognises me for what I am! Oh!
had I but one friend, or even an enemy, to whom I could
betake myself, and be known as the vilest of sinners. Even
thus much truth would save me, for now all is falsehood
and emptiness!

Hester. Such a friend as thou hast even now wished for,
with whom to weep over thy sin, thou hast in me, the
partner of it!—(Hesitating.) Thou hast long had such an
enemy,—and dwellest with him,—under the same roof!

Dimmesdale. Ha! what sayest thou, an enemy! and under
mine roof! What sayest thou?

Hester. Oh, Arthur forgive me! In all things else I
have striven to be true! Truth was the one virtue which
I might have held fast, and did hold fast through all extremity; save when thy good,—thy life,—thy fame, were
put in question! Then I consented to a deception. But
a lie is never good, even though death threaten on the
other side! Dost thou not see what I would say?—That

old man!—Thy physician!—he whom they call Roger Chillingworth!—he was—my husband!

Dimmesdale. Merciful God! (Staggers and sinks down upon the rock at R.) I might have known it! I did know it! Oh! Hester, thou little knowest the horror and ugliness of this exposure of a guilty heart to the very eyes that would gloat over it! Woman, I can never forgive thee!

Hester. But thou wilt forgive me! (Falls upon her knees beside him.) Here at thy feet thou shalt forgive me! Let God punish! but, Arthur, thou must forgive me!

Dimmesdale. Hester, I do forgive thee, and may God forgive us both! We are not the worst sinners in this world. There is one worse even than the polluted priest! The old man's revenge has been blacker than my sin. He has violated in cold blood, the sanctity of a human heart. But here is a new horror for me. Will Chillingworth keep my secret?

Hester. There is a strange secrecy in his nature that has grown upon him by the hidden practices of his revenge. He will doubtless seek other means of satiating his dark passion.

Dimmesdale. How am I to dwell longer with this deadly enemy? Think for me, Hester! Thou art strong. Resolve for me!

Hester. Thou must dwell no longer with this man. Thy heart must be no longer under his evil eye!

Dimmesdale. It were worse than death!—But how to avoid it!

Hester. Is the world then so narrow? Doth the universe lie within the compass of yonder town, which only a little time ago was but a leaf-strewn desert, as lonely as this around us? Whither leads yonder forest-track? Backward to the settlement, thou sayest? Yes; but onward too! Deeper it goes, and deeper, into the wilderness, less plainly to be seen at every step; until some few miles hence, the yellow leaves will show no vestige of the white man's tread. There thou art free! So brief a journey would bring thee from a world where thou hast been most wretched, to where thou mayest be most happy! Is there

not shade enough in all this boundless forest to hide thy
heart from the gaze of Roger Chillingworth?

Chillingworth. (Looking from behind the rocks.) Indeed there
is not! (Aside.)

Dimmesdale. Yes, Hester, but only under the fallen leaves!

Chillingworth. Even there I'll see thee! (Aside.)

Hester. Then there is the broad pathway of the sea! It
brought thee hither. If thou so choose, it will bear thee
back again. In our native land, whether in some remote
village, or in vast London,—or, surely in Germany, in
France, in pleasant Italy, thou wouldst be beyond his
power and knowledge! And what hast thou to do with
all these iron men, and their opinions? They have kept
thy better part in bondage too long already!

Dimmesdale. Hester, it cannot be!

Hester. Thou art crushed under this seven year's weight
of misery,—but thou shalt leave it all behind thee! It
shall not cumber thy steps, as thou treadest along the forest-path, neither shalt thou freight the ship with it, if thou
prefer to cross the sea. Leave this wreck and ruin where
it happened? There is good to be done! Begin the
world anew! the future is full of trial and success! There
is happiness beyond. Be a scholar and a sage among the
wisest! Preach! Write! Act! Do anything save to
lie down and die! Give up the name of Arthur Dimmesdale, and make thyself another. Why shouldst thou tarry
one other day in the torments that have so gnawed into
thy life!—that have made thee feeble to *will* and to *do*!
That will leave thee powerless even to repent! Up and
away!

Dimmesdale. Alone, Hester?

Hester. Thou shalt not go alone! I, too, would pluck
this sad symbol from my person! The ship even now lies
in yonder waters, and ere to-morrow's eve, sets her white
sails, which shall be as angel's wings bearing us to a place
of bliss. Look not back! Oh! look not back! that way
lies darkness and death! Pearl! Pearl! Thou shalt see
and know our little Pearl! This way, Pearl! (Enter Pearl
running. Hester hastily places her upon her knees, who clings around

the legs of Dimmesdale looking up into his face.) See, Pearl, the minister! He shall be thy father! Arthur, see and love her as thine!

PICTURE, (Dimmesdale takes up Pearl and kisses her, sits her down— places his hand upon her head, drops upon his knees embracing the child. Hester stands behind them with her hands extended over them in the act of blessing.)

Hester. Bless them, God! Oh, bless them! (At this moment Chillingworth looks from behind the rock, while Hibbins comes from behind the tree, and cautiously observes the situation. She then makes her exit L. 3rd E. During the latter part of the scene, the sun has made its descent on the back flat, and from the horizon throws its crimson rays through the woods, illuminating the stage with a crimson glow. Music, Curtain.)

ACT IV.

Scene First. (In one.)

A room in Dimmesdale's house.   Dimmesdale enters C. D.

Dimmesdale. A night of wild and mixed thoughts have preluded the difficult task I must perform to-day.   Since I parted with Hester, an over-active brain has presented temptations never before mine.   Sin-stained and sorrow-eaten, I flung myself upon the forest leaves, and arose as it were at the entrance of a new life!—This is my last day in Boston, and the last sermon I shall ever preach.—(Enter Hibbins L. E, dressed in a rich velvet gown, high head-dress and yellow, starched ruff of the times.)

Hibbins. A bright morning, good Reverend Master Dimmesdale, and a prosperous end to your work of to-day. The people are all astir.   They expect great things in your Election sermon.   But, indeed, methinks you look brighter for your visit to the forest last night.   The next time you go, I pray you to allow me only a fair warning, and I shall be proud to bear you company.   Without taking too much upon myself, my word will go far toward gaining a quick reception with a certain fair one.

Dimmesdale. I profess, madame, on my conscience I am utterly bewildered as touching the purport of your words! I went not into the forest to seek a fair one, neither do I at any future time design to visit thither.   My one sufficient object was to greet that pious friend of mine, the Apostle Eliot, and rejoice with him over the many souls he hath won from heathendom!

Hibbins. Ha! ha! ha!—well—well, we must needs talk thus in the day-time!   Ha! ha! ha! you carry it off like an old hand.   But, my reverend Sir! be not too sure of the morrow!   We may yet meet in the forest with mutual understanding.   Well, and heaven be with thee, may this day's work end as thou designest.   Keep a stout heart, and perhaps a white signal may wave to thee as a friendly

parting. A stout heart, Master Dimmesdale, and success!
(Exit L.)

Dimmesdale. Have I then sold myself to the fiend, whom,
if men say true, this yellow-starched and velvety old hag
has chosen for her prince. What is she that haunts me
thus, and tells me of things, I thought that none but one
other knew of. Am I mad! (A knock at C. D.) Come in!
(Enter Chillingworth.)

Chillingworth. Welcome home, Reverend Sir, and how
found you that godly man, the Apostle Eliot? But, methinks dear sir, you look pale; as if the travel through the
wilderness had been too sore for you. Will not my aid
be required to put you in heart and strength to preach
your Election sermon?

Dimmesdale. Nay. I think not so, my journey yonder
and the breathing of the free air has done me good. I
think to need no more of your drugs, good though they
be, and administered by a friendly hand.

Chillingworth. Verily, dear sir, we must make youstrong,
for on this occasion you have an extra task to perform.
The people look for great things, and apprehend that another year may come about and find their pastor gone.

Dimmesdale, Kind sir, my present frame of body needs
not your aid.

Chillingworth. I joy to hear it! It may be that my reme-
dies so long administered, begin now to make due effect.
Happy man were I, and well deserving of New-England's
gratitude, could I achieve your cure!

Dimmesdale. I thank you, *most watchful friend*, and can
but requite your good deeds with my prayers.

Chillingworth. A good man's prayers are a golden recom-
pense.

Dimmesdale. They are the current gold coin of the new
Jerusalem, with the King's own mint mark on them!

Chillingworth. A *good* man's prayers.

Dimmesdale. I meant so.

Chillingworth. A man without deceit, one whose life is
not a lie, and who is what he seems.

Dimmesdale. There are such. (Turns away.)

Chillingworth. He blanches and turns away. (Aside.) This is a busy day with thee, and I will not rob thee of time. I will leave thee to thy thoughts. Heaven may see fit to transmit through the *good* man's mouth the grand and solemn music of its oracles! I humbly take my leave, Master Dimmesdale. (Bows very low. Exit C. D.)

Dimmesdale. The hour is not far distant when I shall be separated eternally from thee. There is a strange and solemn beating about my heart, that fills me with dark foretellings,—a whispering that I shall not go! These thoughts will never do! I must not clog up my path to the result with frightful phantoms born of an over-wrought brain. The task must be performed, and the swelling billows of the ocean to-night must cradle my brain to a restful sleep.—(Exit R. F. E.)

SCENE TWO.

MARKET-PLACE.

The same as the second scene in the first act. Flags, banners, and streamers are hanging in all directions across the top of the stage, and from the windows of the buildings, in celebration of Election-day. Crowds of all kinds of people fill the stage. Two men in armor are fencing, upon the platform of the pillory. Indian boys are shooting at a target with bows and arrows. At R. C, below the City Hall, is a large Punch and Judy Box at work, with a group of men, women, and children laughing at the performance. At left C., above 2d E, are two Indians tussling. The laughing, fencing, and tussling continue in action for a few minutes after the curtain is up. All of the characters are kept in action during the rest of the scene, without interfering with the dialogue. Chillingworth discovered leaning against one of the columns of the City Hall. Hester enters with Pearl, from L. H. 3rd E, and comes down to C.

Pearl. Why, mother, what is this? Is it a play-day for the whole world? See there is the blacksmith with a clean face, and little Sue has shoes on. Do tell me, what is to-day?

Hester. This is a Holiday. The people wait to see the

procession with the Governor, the great folks and soldiers with music at their head, who will all go into the Town Hall to hear the minister preach his Election sermon.

Pearl. And will the minister hold out both hands to take me, and kiss me as he did in the forest?

Hester. He will see thee, my child, but he will not take thee as in the forest, nor must thou greet him as he passes by. There, look about at the strange sights, but go not far. (Pearl wanders about the stage. The crowd call attention to Pearl and her dress. Enter L. U. E, Capt. Goodwill who appears to be looking about for Hester, who stands L. C. in a thoughtful mood.)

Goodwill. So, Mistress Hester, I have found thee at last. I would say to thee, aboard by five o'clock at latest. We shall have other company, and hereabouts I would find my new passenger to give him the same tidings. (Chillingworth observes Goodwill talking to Hester. He looks at Hester with a sarcastic smile.) No fear of scurvy, or ship-fever this voyage, what with the ship's surgeon and this other doctor, our only danger will be from drugs.

Hester. (Startled.) What mean you? Who is this other passenger?

Goodwill. Why know you not, that this Master Chillingworth,—he calls himself,—is minded to try a cabin-fare with you? Ay—Ay, you must have known it, for he tells me he is of your party, and a close friend to the gentleman that is in peril from sickness.—Why, there stands the old doctor himself, smiling at us. (Points at Chillingworth, who looks at Hester. She casts a quick glance at Chillingworth, staggers backward, and is saved from falling by Goodwill.)

Goodwill. Why, my lady, are you not well? Shall I call the old doctor?

Hester. No! no! tis nothing,—a little dizziness,—a habit,—'tis over.—Yes, they know each other well indeed! (Music without.) I must look after my little Pearl, and anon we will speak further of this matter. (Goodwill retires. Pearl comes to Hester, who stands L. C. Procession enters L. F. E. headed by Brackett with staff of office, next band of music, followed by twelve men in armor, next the Governor and Officers of State followed by Dimmesdale alone: after him, Wilson, and several others in minis-

terial gowns, other soldiers, &c., &c. The procession passes into the
City Hall, followed by all the people. The twelve men in armor arrange themselves each side of the City Hall, and each side of the Pillory. Chillingworth and Goodwill enter the City Hall last. Hester
with Pearl remain in abstraction at L. C. Hibbins who, disguised, has
been moving around the stage during the whole of the scene, watching
Hester and Chillingworth, now enters L. 2d E, dressed in her rich
gown of velvet, &c.)

Hibbins. Ha! ha! Mistress Hester, a great day for the
City of Boston. Town and country all here. The red
heathen and the white Christian all mingle together. But
what mortal imagination could conceive it! that yonder
Divine man, that saint on earth, as the people uphold him
to be, and, I must needs say, really looks! who now that
saw him pass, would think how little time it is since he
went forth out of his study,—chewing a Hebrew text of
scripture in his mouth, I warrant,—to take an airing in
the forest! Aha! we know what that means, Hester
Prynne!

Hester. Well.—

Hibbins. But truly, forsooth, I find it hard to believe him
the same man. Many a church member, too, I saw but
now walking behind the music, that has danced in the
same measure with me, and it might be an Indian, or a
Lapland wizard changing hands with us! But that is a tri-
fle, when one knows the world; yet this minister! couldst
thou surely tell, Hester, whether he is the same man that
encountered thee on the forest-path?

Hester. Insolent meddler! What is it to thee? I tell
thee, audacious woman, that yonder scaffold will never
more fitly have its own 'till you stand there an example of
your dark ways!—Begone!

Hibbins. Fie, woman, fie! Dost thou think I have been
to the forest so many times, and have yet no skill to judge
who else has been there? Yes; though no leaf of the wild
garlands they wore, be left behind! I know thee, Hester,
for I behold the token we may all see in the sunshine, and
it glows like a red flame in the dark! Thou wearest it
openly. But this minister! what is it, he seeks to hide
with his hand always over his heart? Ah! Hester Prynne!

Hester. Old woman! the dirt on yonder minister's shoes is cleaner than thy soul!—(A shout of " Make room, make room !" is heard within the Hall. The people rush from the Hall to left side of the stage shouting, " The minister is dying!" Hester shrieks, and with Pearl staggers up to the left side of the pillory steps. Enter from the Hall, Dimmesdale, supported by Bellingham, followed by Chillingworth. Dimmesdale staggers to the steps of the pillory where he sees Hester, grasps her hand.)

Dimmesdale. Hester, come hither! Come, my little Pearl!

Chillingworth. Madman, hold! Do not perish in dishonor!—

Dimmesdale. Thou art too late. With the help of God, *mine* is the power to reveal the truth! Come, Hester! Come! (Dimmesdale, Hester and Pearl ascend the scaffold.) People of New-England! ye that have loved me, ye that have deemed me holy! Behold the one sinner! At last I stand, where seven years since I should have stood, beside this woman. Lo, the Scarlet Letter that Hester wears, is also mine! Our souls are equally bound up in it!—Behold! (Throws open his dress and exposes a Scarlet Letter upon his heart. The crowd shrink back in amazement, all exclaiming as in one voice, " The Scarlet Letter!" Dimmesdale then staggers down the scaffold, followed by Hester and Pearl. He falls F. C, supported by Hester, Pearl at left of Hester.) Is this not better than what we dreamed of in the forest?

Hester. I know not! I know not! Better?—Yes; so we may die, and with us, little Pearl!

Chillingworth, (R. of Dimmesdale.) Thou hast escaped me! But thou art known!

Dimmesdale. Thou, too, hast deeply sinned. May God forgive thee! (Falls back.) Hester, I am dying!—

Hester. Shall we not meet again? Shall we not spend our immortal lives together? Have we not ransomed one another with all this woe? Thou lookest far into eternity,—tell me what thou seest?

Dimmesdale. Hush, Hester, hush! The law we broke!— The sin so awfully revealed! God knows, and he is merciful! (Dies, with his head resting on Hester's bosom. Pearl buries

her face in her hands.   Chillingworth stands R. with his back turned
on Dimmesdale.   Bellingham and Wilson stand immediately behind
Dimmesdale, looking down upon his body.   Hibbins, with the group
of citizens, moves down the stage forming a half circle about the front
group.   They all lean foward to look at Dimmesdale, and, as the curtain descends to low, plaintive music, the people all whisper,

"THE SCARLET LETTER!"

THE END.

www.ingramcontent.com/pod-product-compliance
Lightning Source LLC
Chambersburg PA
CBHW030859260626
47169CB00008B/2602